THE DROUGHT ON ZIAX II

THE DROUGHT
ON
ZIAX II

BY JOHN MORRESSY

ILLUSTRATED BY

STANLEY SKARDINSKI

 WALKER AND COMPANY   NEW YORK

Library of Congress Cataloging in Publication Data

Morressy, John.
  The drought on Ziax II.

  SUMMARY: The Earthmen and the natives of the planet
Ziax join forces to find out why water seems to be
disappearing from the planet.
  [1. Science fiction] I. Title.
PZ7.M82714Dr   [Fic]   77-14651
ISBN 0-8027-6315-4
ISBN 0-8027-6316-2 lib. bdg.

First published in the United States of America
in 1978 by the Walker Publishing Company, Inc.

Published simultaneously in Canada
by Beaverbooks, Ltd., Pickering, Ontario

Trade ISBN: 0-8027-6315-4
Reinf. ISBN: 0-8027-6316-2

Library of Congress Catalog Card Number: 77-14651

Printed in the United States of America
10 9 8 7 6 5 4 3 2 1

CONTENTS

1 THE SEARCHERS

TOREN MALLIXXAN RESTED IN the shade of a gampal tree, talking to his friends. The long summer of Ziax II was nearly over, but the days were still hot. The heat and the talking had made Toren very thirsty. He reached for his canteen, but then he remembered his father's orders. Water was strictly rationed. So he licked his dry lips and thought of the cool waters of Earth.

For someone born in space, Toren knew a great deal about Earth. He read all the material in the Base Library. He studied the maps and globes in the schoolroom at ·Pioneer Base One. Whenever the older Pioneers spoke of their home world, Earth, Toren listened closely to all they said.

The friends who sat with Toren were not humans from the Pioneer Base. They were Imbur, the forest people of Ziax II.

The Imbur had round eyes, and no noses, and six fingers on each hand, but otherwise they looked much like the people from Earth. Their bare arms and legs, and their heads, were covered with soft golden fur. They were a shy and gentle people who lived at peace on their world.

The Imbur dressed differently from the Pioneers. Toren and the·other Pioneers wore a silver coverall and boots, but the Imbur each wore a single loose garment that reached from the shoulders to the knees. Stripes on the garment showed the age and rank of the Imbur who wore it.

Toren spoke to them of the land and water of the Earth. The Imbur all spoke the Earthmen's language, but they did not always understand every word. When Toren spoke of oceans, rivers, and lakes, the Imbur had many questions. He tried to explain.

"An ocean is a huge body of water," he said.

"How can water be a body?" one Imbur asked.

"Well, I don't mean like an Imbur body, or a Pioneer's body. Not *that* kind of body."

"What kind of body, then?" another Imbur asked.

Toren scratched his head and thought for a time. The Imbur were always asking questions like that one. They seemed like very simple questions, but when he tried to answer them, he found that they were not simple at all. Still, he had to try. He did not want them thinking that Earth people were stupid.

"An ocean is so much water that if you were out in the middle of it, you couldn't see anything but water wherever you looked," he explained. "A lake is smaller than an ocean, but still very big."

No one said anything for a moment, then someone asked, "How can humans live in all that water?"

"We live on the land. Fish live in the water," Toren said.

"What is fish?" several Imbur asked at once.

Toren sighed. "Fish are creatures made to live in water. Humans are made to live on the land." He patted the firm ground beside him. "Like this, you know. Land. Solid ground."

The Imbur looked at each other. Toren wondered if they understood. It was hard to tell what an Imbur was thinking, because the expression on an Imbur's face never changed. With their big round eyes, the Imbur always looked surprised.

"Things that live in the water must be

very small," said Rilmat. He was Toren's best friend among the Imbur.

"Some of them are bigger than a sork," Toren said.

The Imbur did not change expression, but they made a high clicking sound that showed their surprise. The sork were the biggest creatures living on Ziax II. They were ferocious and very dangerous. Anything bigger than a sork would be frightening to see.

"How can anything so big live in a tiny trickle of water?" Rilmat asked.

At once, Toren understood why they were confused. They simply could not imagine a large body of water, like an ocean or a lake. Again, he tried to explain.

"Try to think of water that reaches as far in all directions as the gampal forest," he said. "Big creatures could live in that, couldn't they?"

"Where would so much water come from?" one of the Imbur asked.

"Water comes bubbling up from the

ground in little puddles," said another.

"Or it trickles down from the rocks," said a third.

"It's not like that on Earth," Toren said. "Earth is different. On Earth, there's three times as much water as land."

They all looked at him and licked their dry lips. "Then Earth is a very fortunate world," Rilmat said. The rest agreed.

Toren climbed to his feet. He was hot and very thirsty, but they had important work ahead. He held out his hand to help Rilmat.

"Ziax II is a good world, too, Rilmat," he said. "We'll find water soon. If it's out there, we'll find it."

The others moved away to rejoin their search teams. Very softly, so no one could hear, Rilmat said, "Suppose there is no water out there, Toren?"

2 THE THIRSTING WORLD

THE FACT IS, ALL THE INHABIT-
ants of Ziax II were in trouble. The Earth
Pioneers had noticed it first.

During the long summer, the water
supply began to fail. By midsummer, the
Pioneers' crops were dying. No one knew
why.

A solution had to be found quickly. If
the Pioneers' crop failed, the Earthmen
could still survive by eating the fruit of
the gampal tree. That was how the Imbur

16

lived. But the trees were withering, too. If the crops failed and the trees died, everyone on the planet might starve.

Commander Mallixxan, leader of the Earth Pioneers, declared an emergency. He issued strict rules for using the water on hand. He arranged to meet with the leader of the Imbur, hoping that by working together, Imbur and Pioneer could solve their problem.

The leader of the Imbur was called the Ru-Imbur. He and the Earthmen's leader knew one another through their sons. Toren, the Commander's son, was a close friend of Rilmat, the son of the Ru-Imbur.

Commander Mallixxan and the Ru-Imbur met for a long time. The next day, the leaders of both races gathered at the Base. The Watchers, wisest of the Imbur, explained the water sources in the gampal forest. The Pioneer Council showed how the Earthmen obtained and purified water from their wells. They were able to learn much from each other. But after all

17

the meetings, they still had no solution.

The water level fell lower each day. Crops turned yellow, and then brown. The plants withered. In the forest, the gampal trees sagged and wilted. And still no one knew why.

One thing was decided. If the deep wells at Pioneer Base One could not supply water, then new sources had to be found at once. Pioneers and Imbur agreed to form teams to search the forest for water.

The search had to be made on foot. The low-flying skysleds used by the Pioneers moved too fast. An observer in a skimmer, as the skysleds were called, could miss many details of the ground beneath him. Every day, skimmers were used to bring supplies and replacements for the search teams. But the work was slow, and hot, and disappointing.

They had been searching for ten days, so far. They had found nothing. And the water supply kept sinking lower.

3
THE DESTRUCTION OF THE SORK

LATE IN THE DAY, EARTHMEN AND Imbur separated to make camp. The Earth Pioneers pitched tents for the night. The Imbur wove a high enclosure from the living vines of the gampal tree, and slept inside it.

Toren had lived with the Imbur for a time. He liked to sleep as they did, in the open, under the stars. But the Pioneers preferred their tents. The Imbur could not understand how anyone could sleep like this. The Earthmen cut themselves off from the sky and the stars and the cool night breeze. So the two races lived in separate encampments.

Toren saw his father standing alone by the entrance to his tent. The search team leaders had just reported to him. No one had found water. His father looked worried. Toren tried to cheer him up.

"Don't worry, Father. We'll find water soon," he said.

His father sighed. "That's not my only worry, Toren."

"What's the matter? Can I help?" Toren asked.

His father did not answer at once, then he said, "Maybe you can. Come on inside."

They went into the command tent. Commander Mallixxan closed the tent flap behind them, so no one would enter. He and Toren sat in folding chairs.

"I spoke with the Ru-Imbur today, Toren. He's displeased because we've been shooting the sork," Commander Mallix-xan said. "I can't seem to make him understand how dangerous sork are to us."

The sork were not only dangerous creatures, they were fearful to look upon. A full-grown sork was more than twice as tall as a man. It had a gaping mouth full of long teeth. Big bulging eyes with slitted pupils glared from its forehead. It could snap the trunk of a gampal tree in its claws. Sork had killed and injured many Pioneers in the early days of settlement on Ziax II. To protect themselves, the Pioneers had taken to shooting all sork on sight.

The Imbur believed that this was wrong. Imbur had a way of controlling the sork without using weapons. By chanting certain sounds, they could put the creatures into a deep sleep. They tried to teach the Earthmen their chant. But the Earthmen did not trust this method. They felt safer using their weapons. Imbur did not believe in taking

life, and so the use of weapons on the sork troubled them.

"The chant of the Imbur *will* stop the sork, Father. You've seen that for yourself," Toren said.

"Yes, I have. But the men claim that they can't make the chant work as well as the Imbur can. The sounds just don't come naturally to a human throat."

"It isn't easy, Father. But they could learn. I learned it, didn't I?"

"True, you did," Commander Mallixxan admitted. "But you lived among the Imbur. Until the men learn it, they have to protect themselves. I respect the beliefs of the Imbur, son. I don't want them to think of us as savages. But if I must choose between the lives of my people and the lives of sork, then I'll wipe out every sork on Ziax II, if I must."

"Maybe we've already done that," Toren said.

"What do you mean?" his father quickly asked.

"Well, we've been in the forest ten days, and no one has seen a sork. And they haven't been sighted around the Base all summer."

Commander Mallixxan frowned. "You're right, Toren. I hadn't thought of that. What about the Imbur? Have they seen any?"

"No. I asked Rilmat yesterday. He said none of the Imbur have seen a sork for a long time," Toren said.

"I guess that explains why the Ru-Imbur is unhappy. He thinks we've killed all the sork. And maybe we have." Commander Mallixxan laid a hand on his son's shoulder. "Do you still want to help me?" he asked.

"Yes, I do," Toren replied.

"All right, then. Tomorrow, when we split into teams, you go with the Ru-Imbur's group. Talk to him. Let him know how the Pioneers feel. Maybe if he realizes that they're simply acting out of fear, he'll be more understanding. Will you do that for me, son?" Commander Mallixxan asked.

Toren agreed to help in any way he could.

4
UNKNOWING ONES

THE NEXT DAY TOREN WAS PART of a search team that included the Ru-Imbur, Rilmat, and two Pioneers. As they moved off to their designated search area, Toren stayed close to the Ru-Imbur. He was waiting for the chance to talk to him apart from the others.

After a time the Pioneers separated from the others. Toren saw his opportunity to speak.

"My father says that you're displeased

because some of the Pioneers have killed sork," he said.

"You know that the Imbur never take life, Toren," the Ru-Imbur replied.

"But you can use the chant. It works for you. It doesn't work for the Pioneers."

"It would work, if they tried harder."

"But that would take time. What would they do in the meantime for protection?" Toren asked.

"We would help to keep the sork away. But the Pioneers do not ask for our help. They use their weapons instead," the Ru-Imbur said.

"Maybe they just don't trust the chant," Toren said. Quickly, he added, "I do, because I've seen it work. And I've used it myself. But to a Pioneer, it's different. They've learned to trust their weapons."

The Ru-Imbur's voice sounded sad as he spoke. "That is the great problem, Toren. The Pioneers trust only their weapons. Your people may have destroyed the last sork on Ziax II."

Toren felt that the Ru-Imbur did not really understand. He seemed to think that sork were as important as people. Toren said, "What if we have? We saved lives. What good is a sork, anyway? It's just a big ugly thing that destroys everything it sees."

"The sork knows no better. The Earthmen do. To kill the last of any creature is a terrible deed, Toren, whatever the reason."

They walked on for a time without speaking. Toren began to feel ashamed of what he had said. Finally, he asked, "You don't like Earthmen very much, do you?"

The Ru-Imbur halted, stooped down, and placed his hands on Toren's shoulders. This was a special way of communicating that the Imbur sometimes used. Toren had learned it, and other Imbur ways, when he lived among them.

"Toren, you are as close to me as Rilmat is. I admire your father and mother and all the Earth Pioneers. But it troubles me

that even though they hate and fear the sork, the Pioneers act like sork themselves. The sork kills because it is an unknowing one. It cannot help but kill. But the Earthmen have intelligence, and yet they, too, kill," the Ru-Imbur said.

Deep inside Toren's mind, the words seemed to become richer in meaning. For a moment, Toren could feel all the Ru-Imbur's confusion and sadness. He knew that the Ru-Imbur loved the Pioneers, and yet he feared them, too. They solved problems by destroying. That was not the Imbur way. Commander Mallixxan seemed to understand, but he did not stop the killing.

The Ru-Imbur removed his hands, and the images in Toren's mind faded. Toren still sensed the problem, and it troubled him. He wanted so much to help. But he did not know how.

5
THE
TWINING
GRASS

TOREN SLEPT POORLY THAT night. He kept waking up, thinking of the problems facing his father. Somehow, Commander Mallixxan had to find water. He had to figure out a way to bring it back to Pioneer Base One. And he had to prove to the Imbur that Earthmen were not really cruel, only frightened. How could he do all these things?

The next day, as they set out on the search, Toren told Rilmat of his worries. His friend felt sorry for him. Rilmat wanted to help, but could think of no solution.

The search teams traveled deep into the forest. They were now in a region totally unknown to the Pioneers. Few Imbur had ever traveled this far. Here they found no trails or markings to guide them. And still no trace of water.

As they went on, they found the forest changing. The gampal trees were shrunken. The fruit was small and withered. It seemed that the lack of water was even worse here than elsewhere on the planet.

But not all the trees were dying. Some seemed healthy. Their fruit was a bright gold. Toren bit into one of the gampal fruits. It was juicy and delicious, just as it should have been.

Rilmat noticed the same thing. He and Toren studied the trees more closely. They sought some pattern to the healthy and unhealthy ones. When they found a row of very dry, very stunted gampal trees, they followed it to find some clue.

The undergrowth became thicker as they went on. At first it was only a bother. Soon, though, it made the walking difficult. A tangle of pale orange grass was everywhere on the ground. Some of the stalks were as thick as Toren's finger. As the searchers went on, the stalks became longer and higher. When they reached a point where the orange grass was knee-high, Toren stopped. He was hot, and tired, and very thirsty. The walking was very difficult. At every step, the orange grass clung to his boots.

Rilmat, too, was tired. They stopped under a gampal tree. Toren passed his canteen to Rilmat. They both needed a drink of cool water.

When Rilmat had drunk, Toren raised the canteen to his lips. As he started to drink, something tugged at his ankle. Rilmat cried out. The grass was moving all around them. It was closing in. Already, long strands were twined around

Toren's legs. One of Rilmat's arms was encircled.

"What is this stuff, Rilmat?" Toren cried, tugging at the grass.

"I don't know. Help me, Toren!"

Toren tried to pull his feet free, but he could not. The orange grass was climbing higher all around him. One strand closed around his wrist, but he pulled it loose. Another encircled him, then another. He jerked one loose, but two others wrapped around his arm. He shouted as loud as he could, and Rilmat joined his cries. The orange grass kept pulling them down.

Toren felt a stinging in his arms and legs. It was like a lot of tiny needles pricking his skin. He shouted louder, and fought to stay on his feet.

"I can't stay up, Toren! It's pulling me down!" Rilmat cried.

"Try, Rilmat! Help will be here soon!"

"I can't! The tendrils are too strong for me!"

Toren tried to rip his feet free so he

could help his friend. But he was an-chored solidly. Tendrils of the orange grass were wound around his arms and legs. He felt himself being pulled to his knees. With all his remaining strength, he gave one last cry for help.

From far away came the voices of Earthmen. The sound gave Toren new hope. He struggled erect and called again and again. The voices of their rescuers came closer. Rilmat, too, found the strength to resist the pull of the orange strands for a little longer.

Commander Mallixxan burst from the forest. He headed straight for the two boys. As he ran, he drew his machete. With quick slashes, he freed Rilmat and then Toren. Toren was glad that his father had saved Rilmat first.

Once Toren and Rilmat were out of danger, other Pioneers began to slash at the orange grass with their machetes. In a few moments, only stumps of the orange grass could be seen.

"Are you all right, son?" Commander Mallixxan asked.

Toren nodded. He did not want to talk yet. His voice felt shaky. Some tendrils still clung to his sleeve, and he pulled them off. Just touching them made him shiver.

"Let me have those tendrils, Toren," his father said. "We've never seen anything like this. I want to have it analyzed."

"It's awful stuff, Father," Toren said. "I felt it stinging me. It was like a lot of little needles."

"We'll have the doctor look at you and Rilmat right away," Commander Mallixxan said. He helped Toren to his feet. As they turned to leave, they faced the Ru-Imbur.

"You saved my son," the Imbur leader said. " I could not have come in time, or freed him from the growth."

"You saved Toren when he was lost in the forest and injured. I'm glad I could return the deed," Commander Mallixxan said.

The Ru-Imbur stepped back one pace, bowed, and raised his hands to his forehead. He repeated the gesture twice, then let them pass. Other Imbur made the same gesture as Toren and his father went by.

"What are they all doing? Isn't that their way of saying hello and goodbye?" Commander Mallixxan asked his son.

"When they repeat it like that, it's a sign of respect," Toren told him.

"Are you sure?"

"Yes. Rilmat told me so."

His father smiled and put his arm around Toren's shoulder. "It looks as though you helped me win back the Ru-Imbur. But next time, don't try so hard."

6
PIONEER
BASE
ONE

THE EARTHMEN HAD A HOSPITAL and laboratory at Pioneer Base One. Commander Mallixxan brought Toren and Rilmat back on a supply skimmer. The Ru-Imbur remained in charge of the search teams.

Toren still had tiny red marks on his arms when they arrived. But he was not in pain. He felt as good as ever, except for a terrible thirst. Rilmat, too, was very thirsty. Commander Mallixxan gave them all the water he could spare, but it was not nearly enough.

As soon as they landed, the three went directly to the hospital. Doctor Wamukota, Chief Medical Officer of the base, was waiting for them. While Toren and Rilmat were examined, Commander Mallixxan brought the samples of orange grass to the laboratory for analysis.

Doctor Wamukota placed Toren and Rilmat on tables at once. After a quick but thorough examination by machine, she examined them more closely. Her hands were very gentle as she felt the punctures in Toren's arm.

"Will we be all right, Doctor?" Toren asked.

"You appear to be in perfect health," she told him, smiling. "That orange grass didn't do anything but scare you."

"I'm awfully thirsty," Toren said.

"So am I," said Rilmat.

"Well, you can help yourselves to wa-

ter, just this once," Doctor Wamukota told them.

Commander Mallixxan entered the examining room at this point, and heard the good news. He let out a sigh of relief.

"What about those red marks, Doctor?" he asked.

Wamukota shook her head. "I'm not sure about them, Commander. They seem to be fading very quickly and leaving no effect on the boys."

"Are you sure Toren and Rilmat haven't been poisoned in some way?" asked Commander Mallixxan.

"Definitely not," the doctor said. "Nothing has been introduced into their bodies."

Commander Mallixxan was still concerned. "Has anything been taken out? Have they lost any blood?"

"No evidence of it," Doctor Wamukota said. "Their water level is low, but that's probably the result of working in the heat on short water rations."

"They were both very thirsty all the way back here."

When Commander Mallixxan said that, Doctor Wamukota looked very thoughtful, as if an idea had occurred to her. "Wait a minute, Commander—did the thirst begin after you rescued them?"

"Yes. I've never seen them so thirsty," Commander Mallixxan said.

"They still are. They asked for water as soon as I finished the examination. Commander, I think we ought to go to the lab and see what they've learned about that plant."

"Do you think it may be poisonous after all?"

Doctor Wamukota shook her head. "Not poisonous. But it might be very dangerous."

7
THE SECRET OF THE ORANGE GRASS

THE FOUR OF THEM WENT TO-gether to the base laboratory. Toren's mother met them at the entrance. She was in charge of the laboratory.

"Toren and Rilmat are fine," Commander Mallixxan assured her, even before she could ask. "What have you found out about the plant?"

She hugged the two boys and looked them over very closely for herself. When she saw the red marks on Toren's arms, she frowned.

"Don't worry, Mother," he said. "It doesn't hurt. I'm all right. Doctor Wamukota said so."

Taking the boys by the hand, Toren's mother led them into the lab. The others followed. Inside, she said to them, "This is a strange growth. It seems to live only on water. And it can extract water from anything."

Commander Mallixxan looked puzzled. "If it lives on water, how can it be so healthy? This whole planet is drying up."

"I don't know. But look at this."

She cut a tiny piece of the orange grass. Placing it in a glass beaker, she filled the beaker with water. Before their eyes, with a speed that astonished them, the orange grass absorbed all the water. It began to grow in thin, thread-like strands.

"Maybe we're lucky there's a water

shortage. That thing could cover the planet in a very short time," Commander Mallixxan said.

"There's another possibility," Toren's mother said. "The plant might be the cause of the shortage."

"That doesn't make sense," the Commander objected. "If this plant were draining off all the water, we'd see it everywhere. But we've never seen it before."

Rilmat had been silently studying the plant growing in the beaker. In a startled voice, he said, "This is the sorkampal. It *does* grow everywhere on our world!"

Commander Mallixxan said, "Why didn't you say so before, Rilmat?"

"I did not recognize it before. I have never seen it growing so big. This is the size I know," he said, pointing to the thread-like strands in the beaker.

"Then that's the answer," Toren's mother said. "Something has made this plant grow, and now it's big enough to consume the water supply of the entire planet."

Doctor Wamukota said, "But what could have happened? Is it some kind of mutation?"

"No evidence of it," Toren's mother said. She turned to Rilmat. "What did you call the plant, Rilmat?"

"Sorkampal. In your language, that would mean food-of-the-sork."

"Is this really what the sork eat?" Wamukota asked.

"Yes. They feed on the young shoots. So the sorkampal never grows larger than that piece," Rilmat said, pointing to the beaker. "That is why I did not recognize it at first."

"At least now we have an idea what's taking our water. Now, what can we do to reclaim it? Can we boil this stuff, or wring out the water?" Mallixxan asked.

His wife shook her head. "There's no way to reclaim the water. Somehow, this plant breaks water down completely. The only thing to do is control it. We must restore the old balance."

"We can't," Commander Mallixxan said. "We disturbed the old balance, but only the sork can restore it."

"What do you mean, Father?" Toren asked.

"For ages, sork have fed on the orange grass. They ate the young shoots and kept it from growing large enough to disrupt the water supply. But then we came and started killing off the sork."

"So now there's nothing to control the sorkampal!" Toren cried.

Toren's mother looked at the plant in the beaker. "In a short time, that orange grass will cover all of Ziax II. Everything else will die out," she said.

Commander Mallixxan leaned his hands on the laboratory table and lowered his head. When he raised his eyes to look at his wife, Doctor Wamukota, and the two boys, his expression was very sad.

"Only the sork can save us," he said,

"and we may have destroyed the last sork on Ziax II. If we have, then we've destroyed a whole planet, and ourselves with it."

8
THE RU-IMBUR SPEAKS

THAT NIGHT THEY SLEPT AT THE base. Early next morning, Commander Mallixxan took Toren and Rilmat back to the forest.

It was a long ride. Looking down from their skimmer, they could see great patches of withered gampal trees. In one place Rilmat pointed out a patch of sork-ampal. It was almost as high as the trees and covered an area as large as Pioneer Base One. All around it the gampal trees were dead or dying.

Commander Mallixxan gazed down sadly. "It looks even worse from up here, doesn't it?" he said.

"Don't be discouraged, Commander," Rilmat said.

"At least we know what's causing the trouble," said Toren.

Commander Mallixxan nodded his head gravely. "We've caused the trouble. The Earthmen came to Ziax II and wiped out the sork. Without the sork, the orange grass grew out of control. Now it will destroy us all, and there's nothing we can do."

"The Ru-Imbur will find a way," Rilmat said.

"I hope so, Rilmat. It's beyond our power now," Commander Mallixxan admitted.

They traveled most of the day. Near dusk, they saw the base camp of the Ru-

Imbur's search teams. Commander Mallixxan had sent word to all the others to join them here. Most of the Imbur and Pioneers were now assembled, awaiting the Pioneer Commander's arrival.

The Pioneer leaders and the Imbur Watchers met that night. Commander Mallixxan told the whole story to the group. When he was finished, those present began to offer their suggestions.

Some felt that Pioneers and Imbur should migrate to the far side of the planet. Others wanted to refit the spaceship that had brought the Pioneers to Ziax II from Earth. They hoped that the two races could find a new world together. But few people thought that these ideas would work.

"Let's get together and find a way to destroy this sorkampal. That's our enemy," said one Pioneer.

Other Pioneers agreed with him. The Imbur were displeased. A Watcher rose to object.

"The sorkampal must not be destroyed," he said. "Its roots go deep, and help to hold the soil of our forest together."

Another Watcher said, "The sorkampal helps to draw water to the dry places of our planet. Destroy it, and the gampal forest will become a desert."

"It will become a desert a lot faster if we don't!" the Earthman cried.

Commander Mallixxan raised his hands for order. Everyone was quiet. He spoke then, and his voice was low. He sounded very sad.

"Destroying the sorkampal or anything else won't help now," he said. "If we hadn't been so quick to destroy, we wouldn't be in trouble now. The Imbur warned us not to harm the sork. We didn't heed their warning. Now we find that the sork is necessary on this planet, just like the sorkampal. Living things are all related. They all depend on one another, in ways we don't always understand. No one has the right to destroy them. But we've learned our lesson too late. Because of the Pioneers, all on Ziax II are doomed."

"Perhaps not," said the Ru-Imbur.

Everyone turned to him. "What hope can there be?" a Pioneer asked.

"Perhaps the sork are not extinct. Perhaps they have only fled to a safer part of Ziax II," the Ru-Imbur replied.

"We've covered a lot of this planet in our search for water. Not one sork has been sighted," Commander Mallixxan said.

"There is one place we have not looked. No one has gone beyond the mountains," the Ru-Imbur said.

"They're sheer cliffs. The skimmers can't go there, because the wind is too strong," one of the Pioneers said.

The Ru-Imbur looked at the Pioneer who had spoken. "And so the sork might have gone there, where his enemies cannot follow."

"That's a long chance to take," the Pioneer said.

"It will be very dangerous," said a Watcher.

Commander Mallixxan stepped to the side of the Ru-Imbur. His voice was no longer low and sad. Now he spoke like a leader.

"All of you are right," he said. "The sork may be beyond the mountains. It *is* a long way, and a long chance to take. It *will* be dangerous. But what choice do we have?"

One of the Pioneers objected, "We came out to hunt water, sir. We're not prepared."

"I'll send the skimmers back for everything we need. Now we're going to hunt sork. This time, we want to save them."

9

THE

HUNT

THE SKIMMERS WERE SENT BACK to Pioneer Base One that very night. By late the next day, they began to return. Every skimmer that could fly was ordered to the assembly point. They came loaded down with food and equipment for Pioneers and Imbur.

Days of planning and long meetings followed. Everyone was busy. At last the preparations were complete. Early one morning, a great fleet of skimmers lifted from the clearing deep in the forest. In close formation they headed for the polar mountain range. No one had ever crossed that range before. Now if they were to save their planet, Pioneer and Imbur had to go where they had never dared to go before.

The skimmers traveled at top speed. For two full days the gampal forest sped by beneath them. Toren and Rilmat stayed by the side of their skimmer, looking at everything below. They saw what appeared to be a stream bed and a small pond. Both were dry and filled with the orange grass. Commander Mallixxan saw these things, too, and he turned away and said nothing. But he was not an Imbur. Toren could read his expression. He could tell that his father was worried. The water that might have saved them was not being found.

Late on the second day of travel they passed the last of the gampal trees. These were small and stunted and very wide

apart. Now the ground was bare beneath them, except for large patches of the orange grass.

They saw the peaks of the mountain range rising far away. Another full day of travel brought them to the foothills. By this time, the winds were getting strong. The skimmers were difficult to control.

Commander Mallixxan ordered them to fly lower. The formation spread out for greater safety. They flew so close to the ground that Toren felt as if he could reach down and touch it. Still the winds grew stronger. When two skimmers nearly collided, Commander Mallixxan ordered all to land. From this point, they would travel on foot.

They set up their base camp where they landed. Commander Mallixxan had brought enough tents for everyone. Even though they did not like to sleep enclosed in a tent, the Imbur were satisfied to use them now, in this part of Ziax II. The wind was cold and penetrating. There

were no gampal trees here to provide vines for weaving shelter. No one knew what kind of creatures might come upon them during the night. A tent was shelter and protection.

Scouting parties went out the next day. Toren and Rilmat were ordered to stay at the base camp. They were unhappy, but they did not argue. The scouts would be out only for a little while, then they would come back to report. The important thing was to go with the main search team.

After they had eaten, Toren and Rilmat went to the edge of the camp and looked at the landscape. The sheer rock rose before them like a wall. There seemed to be no way to climb over those cliffs, and no way to get through. If this were so, could any sork have made it past them, Toren wondered. Perhaps they had come all this way for nothing.

One by one the scouting parties returned. All had bad news. The mountain face was sheer, they said. No pass could be found. Some thought that a skimmer might make it to the top, but it would be blown out of control before it could land.

And then one scouting party returned with good news. They had found a pass to the other side. At the entrance to the pass, they saw traces of sork.

When they heard this news, Pioneers and Imbur began to shout for joy. Toren and Rilmat joined in the shouts. Suddenly Toren began to laugh. The sork had long been their worst enemy on the planet, and now they were cheering to learn it still survived! But the sork, they had learned, was an enemy no longer. It was part of the life of Ziax II. It was necessary. It was a friend.

10 THE RESCUE

THE LEADERS WENT FIRST through the pass. Other Pioneers and Imbur followed them. Toren and Rilmat were almost the last ones to go through.

When they finally came to the far opening, the sight of the others was a surprise. Everyone looked very serious and sad. Toren heard them speak of their disappointment. He looked over the ridge before him, and down into the valley beyond. The sorkampal was everywhere. He saw no ice or snow, even though it was cold here. The sorkampal had absorbed all the moisture from the air.

Toren went to his father. Commander Mallixxan put his arm around his son's shoulder, but said nothing.

"Does this mean the sork are all gone?" Toren asked.

Commander Mallixxan nodded his head. He looked around at his men and the Imbur and the two boys. "The sork is extinct," he said. "Soon the sorkampal will cover all of Ziax II. We can't control it and we can't destroy it. We have no way to reclaim the water it absorbs. We've destroyed a world and its people."

The Ru-Imbur stepped to his side. "You must not say that. As long as we live, we can hope. Let us . . . ."

A loud roar shook the ground, drowning out the Ru-Imbur's words. Another roar followed, even louder. Then came the sounds of struggle, of loud crashing and ripping of sorkampal.

"A sork!" Commander Mallixxan cried.

"Many sork!" shouted the Ru-Imbur.

The leaders gave orders. Earthmen and Imbur quickly moved into formation and started cutting a path towards the sounds. The noise grew louder and more frightening as they came closer. It sounded as though an army of sork were in a great battle.

The searchers came upon six of the creatures. Two sork were full-grown, and the others were small. They were surrounded by sorkampal stalks taller than the tallest gampal trees. The stalks were closing in on the beasts, as they had done to Toren and Rilmat. The sork were tearing at the stalks with their great claws and teeth. But the sork were slowly being overpowered. One small sork, about the size of a calf, had been pulled to the ground. It was squealing in pain and fright. The adult sork were trying to reach it, but they, too, were entangled in the thick stalks. The sorkampal was too strong for them.

The Earthmen moved forward in a line, slashing at the sorkampal with their machetes. The Imbur stayed close behind them. Working furiously, the Pioneers cleared a path to the sork's side, then stopped.

The sork turned their attention to the humans. As long as the orange stalks held them pinned, they could do no harm. But they had to be freed. Commander Mallixxan looked to his men, then to the Ru-Imbur. The leader of the Imbur signalled his readiness.

At Commander Mallixxan's order, the entire party of Pioneers moved ahead at once. They cut away the last strands of sorkampal. Once the sork were free, the Earthmen quickly fell back. Now the Imbur moved forward.

At first, the sork were stunned. Then they turned to attack the intruders. But the Imbur had already begun their sork chant. The huge beasts roared a warning, then rushed at the chanting Imbur. The

Imbur stood their ground. The sork staggered, roared weakly, and stumbled. Then they fell and lay still, in a deep sleep.

11
WORKING
TOGETHER

THE HARDEST PART OF THE whole journey was carrying the sork back to camp. After that, each sork was placed on a skimmer to be brought back to Pioneer Base One as soon as possible.

Toren and Rilmat rode with Commander Mallixxan in a small, fast skimmer. They carried with them one of the baby sork. Toren felt just a little bit uneasy about their passenger. True, the sork was smaller than he was. And it was sleeping peacefully. But it had teeth and claws and big slitted eyes, just like a full-grown adult. And big or small, it was a *sork*. Rilmat acted uneasy, too.

Commander Mallixxan noticed the two of them sitting on the opposite side of the skimmer from the sork. He went over and sat down beside them.

"Is everything all right?" he asked.

"Oh, yes. Everything is fine," they said.

"You aren't worried about anything, are you?"

"Well . . . the sork . . . " Toren said uncomfortably.

"That little fellow? He won't give us any trouble. If he moves, you can quiet him down with the chant," Commander Mallixxan said.

Toren and Rilmat looked at each other. They trusted the sork chant, but still, a skimmer is a very small place to share with a sork. Even a very small, sleepy sork.

"I'm surprised at the two of you," Commander Mallixxan said, smiling good-naturedly at them. "We know the sork chant works. All the Pioneers are willing to trust it now. We had to depend on it back there and it worked perfectly."

"That was awfully close," Toren said, remembering the rescue.

"It was. The timing had to be perfect. It was risky, but it had to be done that way," his father said.

Rilmat asked, "Why didn't we put the sork to sleep first, so the Pioneers would be safe?"

"We couldn't, Rilmat. The sork had to be awake and fighting until the very last minute. It was the only way we could save them all."

Toren nodded. "And every one of them counts, now."

"It certainly does," his father agreed. "We'll release them as soon as we land. In a very short time, they'll have the sork-ampal under control."

"Is there a chance that we might have to rescue them again?" Rilmat asked.

"Yes. That's a real danger," said the Commander. "We'll have to keep a guard on them until we're sure they're safe. The Ru-Imbur and I will see to that. We'll have to work closely from now on."

"It seems funny," Toren said. "First we nearly wipe the sork out, and then we turn around and risk our lives to save it and protect it."

"We've been very lucky. We learned something important about our planet. And it's time we learned something else, too."

"What else?" Toren and Rilmat asked.

"The sork chant," Commander Mallixxan said. "We'll never use a weapon against the sork again. But until they become tame—and that might be a long time—we have to protect ourselves. The Ru-Imbur and I have talked it over, and we feel that you two would be the best ones to teach us. How about it?"

"We can do it," Rilmat said.

"In fact," Toren said, looking at the sleeping sork, "as soon as that fellow starts to move, we'll begin the first lesson!"

THE AUTHOR

John Morressy has written several adult science fiction novels, including *Starbrat* and *Nail Down the Stars*. He is an English professor and is currently serving as Visiting Lecturer in Creative Writing at the University of Maine in Orono. *The Drought of Ziax II* is a sequel to *The Humans of Ziax II*.

THE ARTIST

Stanley Skardinski is a graduate of Rochester Institute of Technology and holds a Master's degree in Graphic Arts from Pratt Institute in Brooklyn. Besides working as a free-lance illustrator and designer, he collects antiques and refurbishes old houses.